Percy B. Shelley, Thomas J. Wise

Letters from Percy Bysshe Shelley to J. H. Leigh Hunt

Volume 1

Percy B. Shelley, Thomas J. Wise

Letters from Percy Bysshe Shelley to J. H. Leigh Hunt
Volume 1

ISBN/EAN: 9783337388034

Printed in Europe, USA, Canada, Australia, Japan

Cover: Foto ©Andreas Hilbeck / pixelio.de

More available books at **www.hansebooks.com**

LETTERS

FROM

PERCY BYSSHE SHELLEY

TO

J. H. LEIGH HUNT

Edited by Thomas J. Wise

IN TWO VOLUMES

VOL. I.

London: Privately Printed.

1894.

THE IMPRESSION

CONTENTS.

VOL. I.

CONTENTS.

NOTE.

This volume contains every known letter addressed by Shelley to Leigh Hunt, whether published previously or not. The manuscripts of most of those which have already been published are fortunately still preserved—some of them are in my own collection of Shelleyana—and, with one or two exceptions only, the letters have here been printed from the original holographs. It is well known that Hunt "sub-edited" such of the letters as were published by himself in his Autobiography *and other works—in some instances he considerably garbled them. Whenever, therefore, any variation is found between the present text of any letter, and the version put forth by Hunt, the reading here given may be accepted as the correct one.*

T. J. WISE.

LETTERS.

B

LETTERS TO LEIGH HUNT.

LETTER I.

UNIVERSITY COLLEGE,
OXFORD.
March 2nd, 1811.
[*Saturday.*]

SIR,

Permit me, although a stranger, to offer my sincerest congratulations on the occasion of that triumph* so highly to be prized by men of liberality; permit me also to submit to your consideration, as one of the most fearless

* The failure of a Government prosecution against *The Examiner.*

enlighteners of the public mind at the present time, a scheme of mutual safety and mutual indemnification for men of public spirit and principle, which, if carried into effect, would evidently be productive of incalculable advantages. Of the scheme, the enclosed is an address to the public, the proposal for a meeting; and shall be modified according to your judgment, if you will do me the honour to consider the point.

The ultimate intention of my aim is to induce a meeting of such enlightened, unprejudiced members of the community, whose independent principles expose them to evils which might thus become alleviated; and to form a methodical society, which should be organized so as to resist the coalition of the enemies of liberty, which at present renders any expression of opinion on matters of policy dangerous to individuals. It has been for the want of societies of this nature that corruption has attained the height at which we behold it ; nor can any of us bear in mind the very great influence which, some years since, was gained by *Illuminism*, without considering that a society of equal extent might establish *rational liberty* on as firm a basis as that which would have supported the visionary schemes of a completely equalized community.

Although perfectly unacquainted with you privately, I address you as a common friend to *liberty*, thinking that, in cases of this urgency and importance, etiquette ought not to stand in the way of usefulness.

My father is in Parliament ; and, on attaining twenty-one, I shall, in all probability, fill his vacant seat. On account of the responsibility to which my residence in this university subjects me, I, of course, dare not publicly avow all that I think ; but the time will

come when I hope that my every endeavour, insufficient as they may be,
will be directed to the advancement of
liberty.

I remain, Sir,
Your most obedient servant,
P. B. SHELLEY.

To Leigh Hunt, Esq.,
London.

LETTER II.

MARLOW.
December 8th, 1816.
[*Sunday.*]

I HAVE received both your letters yesterday and to-day, and I accuse myself that my precipitancy should have given you the vexation you express. Your letters, however, give me unmingled pleasure, and that of a very exalted kind. I have not in all my intercourse with mankind experienced sympathy and kindness with which I have been so affected, or which my whole being has so sprung forward to meet and to return. My communications with you shall be such as to

attempt to deserve this fortunate distinction. Meanwhile, let me lay aside
preliminaries and their reserve ; let
me talk with you as with an old
friend.

First, I will answer your questions.
By some fatality I have seen every
Examiner, but that of last week.
Since I received your letter yesterday,
I have made every exertion to get a
sight of it, unsuccessfully. All the
people who take it in here have for-
warded it to their friends at a distance.
I hear there is one at a village five
miles off; as it is very uncertain
whether I shall be able to procure it, I
will accept your kind offer of sending
it to me. I take in the *Examiner*
generally, and therefore will not trouble
you to send your own copy.

Next, will I own the *Hymn to Intel-
lectual Beauty?* I do not care—as you
like. And yet the poem was composed under the influence of feelings

which agitated me even to tears, so that I think it deserves a better fate than the being linked with so stigmatised and unpopular a name (so far as it is known) as mine. You will say that it is not thus, that I am morbidly sensitive to what I esteem the injustice of neglect—but I do not say that I am unjustly neglected, the oblivion which overtook my little attempt of *Alastor* I am ready to acknowledge was sufficiently merited in *itself;* but then it was not accorded in the correct proportion considering the success of the most contemptible drivellings. I am undeceived in the belief that I have powers deeply to interest, or substantially to improve, mankind. How far my conduct and my opinions have rendered the zeal and ardour with which I have engaged in the attempt ineffectual, I know not. Self love prompts me to assign much weight to a cause which perhaps has none. But thus much I do not seek to conceal from myself, that I am an outcast from human society ; my name is execrated by all who understand its entire import, —by those very beings whose happiness I ardently desire. I am an object of compassion to a few more benevolent than the rest, all else abhor and avoid me. With you, and perhaps some others (though in a less degree, I fear) my gentleness and sincerity find favour, because they are themselves gentle and sincere : they believe in self-devotion and generosity, because they are themselves generous and self-devoted. Perhaps I should have shrunk from persisting in the task which I had undertaken in early life, of opposing myself in these evil times and among these evil tongues, to what I esteem misery and vice ; if I must have lived in the solitude of the heart. Fortunately my domestic circle incloses that within it which compensates for the

loss. But these are subjects for con-
versation, and I find that in using the
privilege which you have permitted
me of friendship, I have indulged in
that quantity of self-love which only
friendship can excuse or endure.

When will you send me your poems?
I never knew that you had published
any other than *Rimini*, with which I
was exceedingly delighted,—the *story*
of the poem has an interest of a very
uncommon and irresistible character,
—though it appeared to me that you
have subjected yourself to some rules
in the composition which fetter your
genius, and diminish the effect of the
conceptions. Though in one sense I
am no poet, I am not so insensible to
poetry as to read *Rimini* unmoved.—
When will you send me your other
poems?

Peacock is the author of *Headlong
Hall*,— he expresses himself much
pleased by your approbation—indeed

it is approbation which many would
be happy to acquire! He is now
writing *Melincourt* in the same style,
but, as I judge, far superior to *Headlong Hall*. He is an amiable man of
great learning, considerable taste, an
enemy to every shape of tyranny and
superstitious imposture. I am now on
the point of taking the lease of a house
among these woody hills, these sweet
green fields, and this delightful river—
where, if I should ever have the happiness of seeing you, I will introduce
you to Peacock. I have nothing to do
in London, but I am most strongly
tempted to come, only to spend one
evening with you; and if I can I will,
though I am anxious as soon as my
employments here are finished to return to Bath.

Last of all—you are in distress for
a few hundred Pounds;—I saw Lord
Byron at Geneva, who expressed for
me the high esteem which he felt for

your character and worth. I cannot
doubt that he would hesitate in contri-
buting at least £100 towards extri-
cating one whom he regards so highly
from a state of embarrassment. I
have heard from him lately, dated
from Milan; and as he has entrusted
me with one or two commissions, I do
not doubt but my letter would reach
him by the direction he gave me. If
you feel any delicacy on the subject,
may I write to him about it? My
letter shall express that zeal for your
interests which I truly feel, and which
would not confine itself to these barren
protestations if I had the smallest
superfluity.

My friend accepts your *interest* and
is contented to be a Hebrew for your
sake. But a request is made in return
which in courtesy cannot be refused.
There is some little luxury, some en-
joyment of taste or fancy you have
refused yourself, because you have not

felt, through the difficulty of your situation, that you were entitled to indulge yourself in it. You are entreated—and a refusal would give more pain than you are willing to inflict—to employ the enclosed in making yourself a present of this luxury, that may remind you of this not unfriendly contest, which has conferred a value on £5 which I believe it never had before.

Adieu,

Most Affectionately Yours,

P. B. SHELLEY.

I will send you an *Alastor*.

[*Addressed outside.*]
Leigh Hunt, Esq.,
    Vale of Health,
        Hampstead,
            Near London.

LETTER III.

[*December*, 1816.]

* * * * *every one* does me full justice ; bears testimony to the upright-
ness and liberality of my conduct to
her [Harriet].

The above fragment is printed by Dr. Garnett in his
Relics of Shelley, 1862, p. 167.

LETTER IV.

GREAT MARLOW,
June 29th, 1817.
[*Sunday.*]

MY DEAR FRIENDS,

I performed my promise, and arrived here the night after I set off. Everybody up to this minute has been, and continues well.

I ought to have written yesterday; for to-day, I know not how, I have so constant a pain in my side, and such a depression of strength and spirits, as to make my holding the pen whilst I write to you an almost intolerable exertion. This, you know, with me is transitory. Do not mention that I am unwell to your nephew; for the advocate of a new system of diet is held bound to be invulnerable by disease, in the same manner as the sectaries of a new system of religion are held to be more moral than other people; or as a reformed parliament must at least be assumed as the remedy of all political evils. No one will change the diet, adopt the religion, or reform the parliament else.

Well, I am very anxious to hear how you get on; and I entreat Marianne to excite Hunt not to delay a minute in writing the necessary letters, and in informing me of the result. Kings are only to be approached through their ministers; who, indeed, as Marianne shall know to her cost, if she don't take care, are responsible not only for all their commissions, but, a more dreadful responsibility, for all their *omissions.* And I know not who has a right to the title of king, if not according to the Stoics, he to whom the King of kings had delegated the prerogative of lord of the creation.

Let me know how Henry gets on, and make my best respects to your brother and Mrs. Hunt. Adieu.

Always most affectionately yours,

P. B. S[HELLEY].

To
Mr. and Mrs. Leigh Hunt.

LETTER V.

MARLOW.
August 16*th*, 1817.
[*Saturday.*]
[*Written by Mary Shelley.*]

MY DEAR MARIANNE,

In writing your congratulations to Shelley on his birthday did not your naughty heart smite you with remorse? Did you not promise to look at some brooches, and send me the descriptions and prices?—But the 4*th* of August arrived and I had no present!

I am exceedingly obliged to you for the loan of the caps. But a nurse. I have a great aversion to the having a Marlow woman,—but I must be provided by the 20*th*. What am I to do? I dare say Mrs. Lucas is out at present, but she may be disengaged by that time.

I am sorry to observe by your letter that you are in low spirits. Cheer up, my dear little girl, and resolve to be happy. Let me know how it is with you, and how your health is as your time advances. If it were of any use I would say a word or two against your continuing to wear stays. Such confinement cannot be either good for you or the child; and as to shape, I am sure they are very far from becoming.

We are all well here. Our dog, who is a malicious beast whom we intend to send away, has again bitten poor little William without any provocation, for I was with him, and he went up to him to stroke his face when the dog snapped at his fingers. Miss Alba is perfectly well and thriving. She crows like a little cock, although (as Shelley bids me say) she is a hen.

Our sensations of indignation have

been a little excited this morning by
the decision of the master of Chancery.
He says the children are to go to this
old clergyman in Warwickshire, who is
to stand instead of a parent. An old
fellow whom no one knows, and [who]
never saw the children. This is some-
what beyond credibility did we not see
it in black and white. Longdill is very
angry that his proposition is rejected,
and means to appeal from the master
to the Lord Chancellor.

I cannot find the sheet of Mrs. J. W.
I send you two or three things of yours
—the stone cup and the soap-dish
must wait until some one goes up to
town.

I am afraid Hunt takes no exercise
or he would not be so ill. I see however that you go to the play tolerably
often. How are you amused?

The gown must not be dear. But
you are as good a judge as I of what
to give Milly as a kind of payment

from Miss Clifford's mamma for the trouble she has had.

Longdill thought £100 per annum sufficient for both Shelley's children, to provide them with clothes and everything. Why then should we pay £70 for A[llegra]?

The country is very pleasant just now, but I see nothing of it beyond the garden. I am *ennuied* as you may easily imagine from want of exercise which I cannot take. The cold bath is of great benefit to me. By the bye, what are we to do with it? Have you a place for its reception? It is of such use for H[unt]'s health that you ought not to be without it ; we can easily get another. If you should chance to hear of any very amusing book send it in the parcel if you can borrow it from Ollier.

Adieu. Take care of yourself, and do not be dispirited. All will be well one day I do not doubt.

I send you £3.

Shelley sends his love to you all, and thanks for your good wishes and pro- mised present. Pray when is this in- tended parcel to come?

Affectionately yours,

M. W. S[HELLEY].

[*Written by Shelley.*]

I will write to Hunt to-morrow or the day after. Meanwhile kindest remembrances to all, and thanks for your dreams in my favour. Your in- cantations have not been *quite* power- ful enough to expel evil from all re- volutions of time. Poor Mary's book came back with a refusal, which has put me rather in ill spirits? Does any kind friend of yours, Marianne, know any bookseller, or has any influence with one? Any of those good-tempered Robinsons? All these things are affairs of interest and preconception.

You have seen Clarke about this

loan. Well, is there any proposal—
anything in bodily shape? My signa-
ture makes any security infallible in
fact though not in law,—even if they
would not take Hunt's. I shall have
more to say on this.

The while—

Your faithful friend,

P. B. S[HELLEY].

To
Mrs. Hunt.

LETTER VI.

CALAIS.
March 13th, 1818.
[*Friday.*]

MY DEAR FRIEND,

After a stormy but very short voyage we have arrived at Calais, and are at this moment on the point of proceeding. We are all very well, and in excellent spirits. Motion has always this effect upon the blood, even when the mind knows that there are causes for dejection.

With respect to Tailor and Hessy* I am ready to certify, if necessary in a Court of Justice, that one of them said he would give up his [qy. *their*] copyright for the £20 ; and that in lieu of

* Should be "Taylor and Hessey."

that he would accept the profits of
Rimini until it was paid.

Yours ever affectionately,

P. B. SHELLEY.

Pray write to Milan.

[*Written by Mary Shelley.*]

Shelley is full of business, and desires
me to finish this hasty notice of our
safety.   The children are in high
spirits, and very well.   Our passage
was stormy, but very short.   Both
Alba and William were sick, but they
were very good, and slept all the time.
We now depart for Italy, with fine
weather, and good hopes.

Farewell my dear Friend, may you
be happy.

Your affectionate friend,

MARY W. S[HELLEY].

[*Addressed outside.*]
Mr. Leigh Hunt,
13, *Lisson Grove North,*
Paddington,
London.
Angleterre.

LETTER VII.

LYONS.
March 22nd, 1818.
[*Sunday.*]

MY DEAR FRIEND,

Why did you not wake me that night before we left England, you and Marianne? I take this as rather an unkind piece of kindness in you; but which, in consideration of the six hundred miles between us, I forgive.

We have journeyed towards the Spring, that has been hastening to meet us from the south; and, though our weather was at first abominable, we have now warm sunny days, and soft winds, and a sky of deep azure, the

most serene I ever saw.   The heat in
this city to-day is like that of London
in the midst of summer.   My spirits
and health sympathise in the change.
Indeed, before I left London, my
spirits were as feeble as my health, and
I had demands on them which I found
it difficult to supply.

I have read *Foliage:* with most of
the poems I was already familiar.
What a delightful poem *The Nymphs*
is—especially the second part !   It is
truly *poetical*, in the intense and em-
phatic sense of the word.   If six hundred miles were not between us, I
should say what pity that *glib* * was not
omitted, and that the poem is not as
faultless as it is beautiful.   But, for fear
I should *spoil* your next poem, I will
not let slip a word upon the subject.

Give my love to Marianne and her
sister, and tell Marianne she defrauded
me of a kiss by not waking me when

* In the phrase, "the glib sea-flowers."

she went away ; and that, as I have no better mode of conveying it, I must take the best, and ask you to pay the debt. When shall I see you again? Oh, that it might be in Italy ! I confess that the thought of how long we may be divided makes me very melancholy.

Adieu, my dear friends. Write soon.

Ever most affectionately yours,

P. B. S[HELLEY].

To
Leigh Hunt, Esq.

LETTER VIII.

———

SKINNER STREET,
LONDON.
December 7th, 1818.
[*Sunday.*]

DEAR SIR,

It was stated to me yesterday by Mr. James Ogilvie, the Orator, that you had informed him that it was now known from incontestable authority that Milton died embracing the creed of Atheism.

I should take it as a particular favour if you would have the goodness to tell me whether this statement of Mr. Ogilvie is correct; and if so, what is the authority from which you spoke.

If I may so accommodate an expres-

sion of St. Paul, " After the way which
men call Atheism, so worship I the
God of my fathers "—so that the information I seek could not give me any
pain ; nor is it possible I should make
an ill use of it. And whatever I might
hereafter at any time say on the subject,
it could not be necessary to join your
name with it to your annoyance.

    I am, my dear Sir,

      With much regard, yours,

          P. B. SHELLEY.

To
Leigh Hunt, Esq.

LETTER IX.

___

NAPLES.
December 22nd, 1818.
[*Monday.*]

MY DEAR FRIEND,

A letter from you is always so pleasant that one never feels less inclined to complain of the long absence of such a pleasure than at the moment when it is conferred. Neither Ollier's parcel nor any of the letters it contains have arrived. I do confess we had been saying now and then, "Well, this is just like Hunt"—as indeed it was a little; but we never attributed your silence to neglect or want of affection. You don't tell me if your book is published yet, or is about to be published soon. As to my little poem, I can only

lament that it is not more worthy of
the lady whose name it bears; though
it may derive, it cannot confer,
honour on the situation where you
have placed it.

I saw the *Quarterly* at Venice, and
was much pleased with the Review of
Frankenstein though it distorts the
story. As to what relates to yourself
and me, it makes me melancholy to
consider the dreadful wickedness of
heart which could have prompted such
expressions as those with which the
anonymous writer exults over my
domestic calamities, and the perver-
sion of understanding with which he
paints your character. There can be
no doubt, with respect to me, that
personal hatred is intermingled with
the rage of faction. I know that
Southey on one occasion said to a
friend of his that he on his own knowledge knew me to be the *blackest of
villains.* When we consider *who* makes

this accusation, and against *whom*, I
need only rebut such an accusation by
silence and a smile. I thought, indeed,
of writing to Southey; but that, as he
is really guilty, would have only ex-
posed me to misrepresentation, and I
shall on my return seek an opportunity
of expostulating with him in person,
and enquiring by what injury I have
awakened in his heart such dreadful
hatred; and if, indeed, I have injured
him unintentionally, to endeavour to
repair it; and if not, to require that he
should produce his proof of my merit-
ing the appellation he employs. As far
as the public is concerned, it is not for
him whom Southey accuses, but for
him whom all the wise and good
among his contemporaries accuse of
delinquency to all public faith and
honour, to defend himself. Besides, I
never will be a party in making my
private affairs or those of others to be
topics of general discussion. Who can

know them but the actors? And if
they have erred, or often when they
have not erred, is there not pain enough
to punish them? My public character
as a writer of verses—as a speculator
on politics, or morals, or religion—as
the adherent of any party or cause—is
public property; and my good faith or
ill faith in conducting these, my talent,
my penetration, or my stupidity, are all
subjects of criticism. I am almost
certain that Southey, not Gifford, wrote
that criticism on your poems. I never
saw Gifford in my life, and it is impos-
sible that he should have taken a personal hatred to me. Gifford is a bitter
partisan, and has a very muddled head;
but I hear from those who know him
that he is rather a mild man personally,
and I don't know that he has ever
changed sides. So much for myself.
As far as you are concerned, I can
imagine why Southey should dislike
you, as the *Examiner* has been the

crown of thorns worn by this unre-
deemed Redeemer for many years.

Do you ever see Peacock? He will
tell you all about where we go, what we
do or see; and, as I wrote him an
account of these things, I do not like
writing twice over the same things.
There are *two* Italies—one composed
of the green earth and transparent sea,
and the mighty ruins of ancient time,
and aerial mountains, and the warm and
radiant atmosphere which is interfused
through all things. The other consists
of the Italians of the present day, their
works and ways. The one is the most
sublime and lovely contemplation that
can be conceived by the imagination of
man; the other is the most degraded,
disgusting, and odious. What do you
think? Young women of rank actually
eat—you will never guess what—*garlick!*
Our poor friend Lord Byron is quite
corrupted by living among these people;
and, in fact, is going on in a way not

very worthy of him. We talked a good
deal about you, and among other things
he said that he wished you would come
to Italy, and bade me tell you that he
would lend you the money for the
journey (£400 or £500) if you were
prevented by that consideration. Pray
could you not make it in some way
even profitable to visit this astonishing
country? We return to Venice next
Spring. What an inexpressible pleasure
it would give us to meet you there! I
fear (if you will allow me to touch on
so delicate a subject) it would be hardly
possible for you to bring *all* your family,
but you would know best. I should
not wonder if Peacock would join you,
and then the ensuing Spring we would
all return together. Italy has the
advantage of being exceeding cheap,
when you are once there; particularly if
you go to market yourself, otherwise
the cheating makes it approach English
prices. If you are indifferent as to see-

ing France, you may sail from London to Livorno, and we would meet then a month earlier than at Venice. I don't think you need feel at all uncomfortable at accepting Lord Byron's offer, (if *I could* make it, you know that I would not give you this advice) as 'twas very frankly made, and it would not only give him great pleasure, but might do him great service, to have your society. Write to me quickly what you think of this plan, on which my imagination delights itself.

Mine and Mary's love to Marianne and Miss K. and all the little ones. Now pray write directly, addressed as usual to Livorno, because I shall be in a fever until I know whether you are coming or no. I ought to say I have neither good health nor good spirits just now, and that your visit would be a relief to both.

Most affectionately and sincerely your friend,   P. B. S[HELLEY].

Ollier has orders to pay Marianne £5. I owe her part of it, and with the other I wish her to pay £1. 10. 0. to the tailor who made my habit if he calls for it. His charge will be more, but do not pay it him.

[*Addressed outside.*]
  Leigh Hunt, Esq.,
    8, *York Buildings,*
      New Road,
        London.
Inghilterra.

LETTER X.

Livorno.
August 15*th*, 1819.
[*Sunday.*]

My Dear Friend,

How good of you to write to us so often, and such kind letters ! But it is like lending to a beggar. What can I offer you in return?

Though surrounded by suffering and disquietude, and latterly almost over-come by our strange misfortune, I have not been idle. My *Prometheus* is finished, and I am also on the eve of completing another work,* totally dif-

* *The Cenci*, printed in Italy towards the close of 1819.

ferent from any thing you might con-
jecture that I should write ; of a more
popular kind ; and, if any thing of mine
could deserve attention, of higher
claims. "Be innocent of the knowledge, dearest chuck, till thou approve
the performance."

I send you a little poem to give to
Ollier for publication, but *without my
name :* Peacock will correct the proofs.
I wrote it with the idea of offering it to
the *Examiner*, but I find it is too long.
It was composed last year at Este :
two of the characters you will recog-
nise ; the third is also in some degree
a painting from nature, but, with respect to time and place, ideal. You
will find the little piece, I think, in
some degree consistent with your own
ideas of the manner in which poetry
ought to be written. I have employed
a certain familiar style of language to
express the actual way in which people
talk with each other, whom education

and a certain refinement of sentiment have placed above the use of vulgar idioms. I use the word *vulgar* in its most extensive sense : the vulgarity of rank and fashion is as gross in its way as that of poverty, and its cant terms equally expressive of base conceptions, and therefore equally unfit for poetry. Not that the familiar style is to be admitted in the treatment of a subject wholly ideal, or in that part of any subject which relates to common life, where the passion, exceeding a certain limit, touches the boundaries of that which is ideal. Strong passion expresses itself in metaphor, borrowed from objects alike remote or near, and casts over all the shadow of its own greatness. But what am I about ? If my grandmother sucks eggs, was it I who taught her ?

If *you* would really correct the proof, I need not trouble P[eacock], who, I suppose, has enough. Can you take it as a compliment that I prefer to trouble you?

I do not particularly wish this poem to be known as mine; but, at all events, I would not put my name to it. I leave you to judge whether it is best to throw it into the fire, or to publish it. So much for self—*self*, that burr that will stick to one. Your kind expressions about my Eclogue gave me great pleasure; indeed my great stimulus in writing, is to have the approbation of those who feel kindly towards me. The rest is mere duty. I am delighted to hear that you think of us, and form fancies about us. We cannot yet come home.

Most affectionately yours,

P. B. SHELLEY.

LETTER XI.

MY DEAR FRIEND,

At length has arrived Ollier's parcel, and with it the portrait. What a delightful present! It is almost yourself, and we sat talking with it, and of it, all the evening. There wants nothing but that deepest and most earnest look with which you sometimes draw aside the veil of your nature when you talk with us, and the liquid lustre of the eyes. But it is an admirable portrait and admirably expresses you—it is a great pleasure to us to possess it, a pleasure in time of need, coming to us

when there are few others. How we
wish it were you, and not your picture !
How I wish we were with you !

This parcel, you know, and all its
letters, are now a year old — some
older. There are all kinds of dates,
from *March* to *August*, and "your
date," to use Shakspeare's expression,
"is better in a pie or a pudding, than
in your letter."—"Virginity," Parolles
says, but letters are the same thing in
another shape.

With it came, too, Lamb's Works.
I have looked at none of the other
books yet. What a lovely thing is his
Rosamond Gray ! How much knowledge of the sweetest and deepest parts
of our nature in it ! When I think of
such a mind as Lamb's—when I see
how unnoticed remain things of such
exquisite and complete perfection,
what should I hope for myself, if I
had not higher objects in view than
fame ?

I have seen too little of Italy, and of pictures. Perhaps Peacock has shown you some of my letters to him. But at Rome I was very ill, seldom able to go out without a carriage : and though I kept horses for two months there, yet there is so much to see ! Perhaps I attended more to sculpture than painting, its forms being more easily intelligible than that of the latter. Yet, I saw the famous works of Raffaele, whom I agree with the whole world in thinking the finest painter. Why, I can tell you another time. With respect to Michael Angelo I dissent, and think with astonishment and indignation of the common notion that he equals, and in some respects exceeds, Raffaele. He seems to me to have no sense of moral dignity and loveliness ; and the energy for which he has been so much praised, appears to me to be a certain rude, external, mechanical quality, in comparison with anything possessed by Raffaele, or even much inferior artists. His famous painting in the Sixtine Chapel seems to me deficient in beauty and majesty, both in the conception and the execution. It might have contained all the forms of terror and delight—and it is a dull and wicked emblem of a dull and wicked thing. Jesus Christ is like an angry pot-boy, and God like an old ale-house keeper looking out of window. He has been called the Dante of painting; but if we find some of the gross and strong outlines which are employed in the most distasteful passages of the *Inferno*, where shall we find *your* Francesca—where the spirit coming over the sea in a boat, like Mars rising from the vapours of the horizon—where Matilda gathering flowers, and all the exquisite tenderness, and sensibility, and ideal beauty, in which Dante excelled all poets except Shakspeare?

As to Michael Angelo's *Moses*—but you have a cast of that in England. I write these things, heaven knows why?

I have written something and finished it, different from anything else, and a new attempt for me; and I mean to dedicate it to you. I should not have done so without your approbation, but I asked your picture last night, and it smiled assent. If I did not think it in some degree worthy of you, I would not make you a public offering of it. I expect to have to write to you soon about it. If Ollier is not turned Jew, Christian, or become infected with *the Murrain*, he will publish it. Don't let him be frightened, for it is nothing which, by any courtesy of language, can be termed either moral or immoral.

Mary has written to Marianne for a parcel, in which I beg you will make Ollier enclose what you know would most interest me—your *Calendar* (a

sweet extract from which I saw in the
Examiner), and the other poems be-
longing to you ; and, for some friends
of mine, my *Eclogue.* This parcel,
which must be sent instantly, will reach
me by October, but don't trust letters
to it, except just a line or so. When
you write, write by the post.

Ever your affectionate,

P. B. S[HELLEY].

[*Addressed outside.*]

    Leigh Hunt, Esq.,

        " *Examiner" Office,*

           19, *Catharine Street,*

                London.

Angleterre.

LETTER XII.

———

LIVORNO.
September 27th, 1819.
[*Monday.*]

MY DEAR FRIEND,

We are now on the point of leaving this place for Florence, where we have taken pleasant apartments for six months, which brings us to the 1st of April, the season at which new flowers and new thoughts spring forth upon the earth and in the mind. What is then our destination is yet undecided. I have not seen Florence, except as one sees the outside of the streets; but its *physiognomy* indicates it to be a city which, though the ghost of a republic, yet possesses most amiable qualities. I wish you could meet us

there in the spring, and we would try
to muster up a " lièta brigata," which,
leaving behind them the pestilence of
remembered misfortunes, might act
over again the pleasures of the Inter-
locutors in Boccaccio. I have been
lately reading this most divine writer.
He is, in a high sense of the word, a
poet, and his language has the rhythm
and harmony of verse. I think him not
equal certainly to Dante or Petrarch,
but far superior to Tasso and Ariosto,
the children of a later and of a colder
day. I consider the three first as the
productions of the vigour of the in-
fancy of a new nation—as rivulets
from the same spring as that which
fed the greatness of the Republics of
Florence and Pisa, and which checked
the influence of the German emperors ;
and from which, through obscurer
channels, Raffaele and Michael Angelo
drew the light and the harmony of
their inspiration. When the second-

rate poets of Italy wrote, the corrupting blight of tyranny was already hanging on every bud of genius. Energy, and simplicity, and unity of idea, were no more. In vain do we seek in the finest passages of Ariosto and Tasso, any expression which at all approaches in this respect to those of Dante and Petrarch. How much do I admire Boccaccio! What descriptions of nature are those in his little introductions to every new day! It is the morning of life stripped of that mist of familiarity which makes it obscure to us. Boccaccio seems to me to have possessed a deep sense of the fair ideal of human life, considered in its social relations. His more serious theories of love agree especially with mine. He often expresses things lightly too, which have serious meanings of a very beautiful kind. He is a moral casuist, the opposite of the Christian, stoical, ready-made, and worldly system of morals. Do you remember one little remark, or rather maxim of his, which might do some good to the common narrow-minded conceptions of love— " Bocca bacciata non perde ventura ; anzi rinnuova, come fa la luna ? "

We expect Mary to be confined towards the end of October. The birth of a child will probably retrieve her from some part of her present melancholy depression.

It would give me much pleasure to know Mr. Lloyd. Do you know, when I was in Cumberland, I got Southey to borrow a copy of Berkeley from him, and I remember observing some pencil notes in it, probably written by Lloyd, which I thought particularly acute. One, especially, struck me as being the assertion of a doctrine, of which even then I had long been persuaded, and on which I had founded much .of my persuasions, as regarded the imagined cause of the universe.—

" Mind cannot create, it can only perceive." Ask him if he remembers having written it. Of Lamb you know my opinion, and you can bear witness to the regret which I felt, when I learned that the calumny of an enemy had deprived me of his society whilst in England.—Ollier told me that the *Quarterly* are going to review me. I suppose it will be a pretty [*paper torn*], and as I am acquiring a taste for humour and drollery, I confess I am curious to see it. I have sent my *Prometheus Un- bound* to P[eacock]; if you ask him for it he will show it you. I think it will please you.

Whilst I went to Florence, Mary wrote, but I did not see her letter.— Well, good b'ye. Next Monday I shall write to you from Florence. Love to all.

Most affectionately your friend,

P. B. S[HELLEY].

To
Leigh Hunt, Esq.

LETTER XIII.

FLORENCE.
November 2nd, 1819.
[*Tuesday.*]

MY DEAR FRIEND,

You cannot but know how sensibly I feel your kind expressions concerning me in the third part of your observations on the *Quarterly ;* I feel that it is from a friend. As to the perverse-hearted writer of those calumnies, I feel assured that it is Southey, and the only notice which it becomes me to take of it, is to seek an occasion of personal expostulation with him on my return to England—not on the ground, however, of what he has written in the *Review,* but on another ground. As to anonymous criticism, it is a much fitter

subject for merriment than serious
comment; except, indeed, when the
latter can be made a vehicle, as you
have done, of the kindest friendship.

Now I only send you a *very heroic*
poem, which I wish you to give Ollier,
and desire him to print and publish
immediately, you being kind enough
to take upon yourself the correction of
the press—not, however, with my name;
and you must tell Ollier that the author
is to be kept a secret, and that I confide in him for this object as I would
confide in a physician or lawyer, or
any other man whose professional situation renders the betraying of what is
entrusted a dishonour. My motive in
this is solely not to prejudge myself in
the present moment, as I have only ex-
pended a few days in this party squib,
and, of course, taken little pains. The
verses and language I have let come as
they would, and I am about to publish
more serious things this winter; after-

wards, that is next year, if the thing should be remembered so long, I have no objection to the author being known, but *not now.* I should like well enough that it should go to press and be printed very quickly ; as more serious things are on the eve of engaging both the public attention and mine.

Next post day you will hear from me again, as I have many things to say, and expect to have to announce Mary's *new work*, now in the press. She has written out, as you will observe, *my* Peter, and this is, I suspect, the last thing she will do before the new birth.

Affectionately yours,

My dear friend,

P. B. S[HELLEY].

To
Leigh Hunt, Esq

LETTER XIV.

FLORENCE.
November 3rd, 1819.
[*Wednesday.*]

MY DEAR FRIEND,

The event of Carlile's trial has filled me with an indignation that will not and ought not to be suppressed.

In the name of all we hope for in human nature what are the people of England about? or rather how long will they and those whose hereditary duty it is to lead them endure the enormous outrages of which they are one day made the victim, and the next the instrument? Post succeeds post and fresh horrors are ever detailed. First we hear that a troop of the enraged master-manufacturers are let loose with sharpened swords upon their starving dependents, and in spite of the remonstrances of the regular troops that they ride over them and massacre without distinction of sex or age, and cut off women's breasts and dash the heads of infants against the stones. Then comes information that a man has been found guilty of some inexplicable crime, which his prosecutors call blasphemy, one of the features of which, they inform us, is the denying that the massacring of children and the ravishing of women, was done by the immediate command of the author and preserver of all things.

And thus at the same time, we see on one hand men professing to act by the public authority who put in practice the trampling down and murdering an unarmed multitude without distinction of sex or age, and on the other, a tribunal which punishes men for asserting that deeds of the same character, transacted in a distant age and country, were not done by the command of God. If not for this, for what was Mr. Carlile prosecuted? For impugning the Divinity of Jesus Christ? I impugn it.—For denying that the whole mass of Hebrew literature is of divine authority? I deny it.—I hope this is no blasphemy, and that I am not to be dragged home by the enmity of our political adversaries to be made a sacrifice to the superstitious fury of the ruling sect. But I am prepared both to do my duty and abide by whatever consequences may be attached to its fulfilment.

It is said that Mr. Carlile has been found guilty by a jury. Juries are frequently in cases of libel illegally and partially constituted, and whenever this can be proved, the party accused has a title to a new trial. A view of the question, so simple that it is in danger of being overlooked from its very obviousness, has presented itself to me, by which, I think, it will clearly appear that this illegal and partial character belonged to the jury which pronounced a verdict of guilty against Mr. Carlile, and that he is entitled to a new trial.

It is the privilege of an Englishman to be tried, not only by a jury, but by a jury of his peers. Who are the peers of any man, and what is the legal import of this word? Let us illustrate the letter by the spirit of the law.

A nobleman has a right to be tried by his peers—a gentleman, a tradesman, a farmer—the like.—The peers of a man are men of the same station, class, denomination with himself. The reason on which this provision is founded, is that the persons called upon to determine the guilt or innocence of the accused, might be so alive to a tender sympathy towards him, through common interest, habits and opinions, as to render it improbable, either that thro' neglect or aversion they would commit injustice towards him, or that they might be incapable of knowing and weighing the merits of the case. Butchers and surgeons are excluded on this ground from juries ; it being supposed by the law that they are engaged in occupations foreign to that delicate sensibility respecting human life and suffering exacted in those selected as arbiters for inflicting it. From the dictation of this spirit, in all cases where foreigners are criminally accused, the jury impanelled are half Englishmen and half foreigners, and the reason why they are not all foreigners is manifest—not that it is theoretically just that any men not strictly his peers should determine between the accused and the country, but because the practical disadvantage arising from the inexperience of foreigners in this admirable form peculiar to English law, would overbalance the advantage of adhering to the shadow, by letting the substance of justice escape. This therefore is the law and the spirit of the law, of juries, and thus plainly and clearly is it illustrated by the ancient and perpetual practice of the English courts of justice.

Who were Mr. Carlile's peers ? Mr. Carlile was a Deist accused of blaspheming the religion of men professing themselves Christians. Who are his peers? Christians? Surely not. Such a proposition is refuted by the very terms of which it is composed. It were to constitute a jury out of the men who are parties to the prosecution —it were to make those who are offended, judges of the cause of him, by whom they profess themselves to have been offended ; it were less absurd to impanel the nearest relations of a murdered man to try the guilt or innocence of a person on whom circumstances attach a strong suspicion of the

deed. No honest Christian would sit
on such a jury except he felt himself
thoroughly imbued with the universal
toleration preached by the alleged
founder of his religion—a state of feel-
ing which we are not warranted by
experience to presume to belong except to extraordinary men. He must
know he could not be impartial. He
sees before him the enemy of his God,
one already predestined to the tortures
of Hell, and who by the most specious
arguments is seducing everyone around
him into the same peril. He probably
feels that his own faith is tottering,
whilst he listens to the prisoner's
defence, and that naturally redoubles
his indignation.—How is such a person
to be considered as the *peer* of the
other, if by peer be meant, one who
from common habits and interests
would be likely to weigh the merits of
the cause dispassionately? He is a
person of the same sect with him who

framed the indictment on which the culprit is accused as a malicious blasphemer. He is evidently less his *peer* with reference to the circumstances of the case than a ploughman would be the peer of a nobleman ; and it is less probable that the one would give an unconscientious verdict from envy towards rank than the other from abhorrence for the speculative opinions of the prisoner.—The Christian may be the peer of the Deist, with reference to any matter not involving a question of his guilt in expressing contumelious sentiments concerning the Christian's own belief (for this, if anything, is meant by blasphemy), because he may have those common interests and feelings which make one man alive to render justice to another ; but with regard to the matter in question he cannot be his peer, because he is one of the persons whom he is charged as having injured, because what he boasts to consider as his most important interests compel him to judge harshly of the accused and impersonate the [accuser ?].   A Quaker's testimony is not indeed admitted in criminal cases, and this disqualification bears with it a sort of appearance of reason.   He protests as it were against the jurisdiction of the court, by refusing to comply with the formality in which it has been the established practice of every British citizen to acquiesce.   Besides, he not only refuses, but refusing, acknowledges the divine authority of that code on which he is nevertheless unwilling to pledge the truth of his statement. This might be interpreted into the leaving himself a loop-hole thro' which to escape. The pretence might be assumed by those who wish to do evil by a false assertion, and yet to escape what they might fear from the vengeance of their God on invocating him as the witness of a deliberate untruth.   At least, all this is plausible. But the truth is that Jesus Christ forbade in the most express terms the attaching to any one asseveration rather than to any other, a sanction to insure its credibility.—This the Quaker knows. The grounds on which the Quaker's testimony is rejected, might be shown to be futile, at present it seems sufficient to have proved, that the same arguments which have been used to exclude the Quaker from his rights (for all civil powers are rights) as a witness and juryman do not apply to the Deist.

On these grounds I think Mr. Carlile is entitled to make application for a new trial, and I am at a loss to conceive how the judges of the King's Bench can refuse to comply with his demands, unless a few modern precedents, founded on an oversight now corrected, are to overturn the very foundations of the law of which they have been perversions. One point of

consideration which was pleaded by
Mr. Carlile on his defence, cannot be
too distinctly understood. The same
justice ought to be dispensed to all.
Of two murderers, one ought not to be
hung, whilst the other having com-
mitted the same crime with the same
evidence notoriously existing against
him, is allowed to walk about at liberty,
—of two perjurers, one ought not to
be pilloried and the other sent on em-
bassies. Nor are they for these real
and not conventional crimes. But is
Mr. Carlile the only Deist ? and Mr.
Paine the only deistical writer that
these heavy penalties are called down
on the person of the one, and these
furious execrations darted from an
indictment upon the works of the other ?
What ! Was Hume not a Deist ? Has
not Gibbon, without whose work no
library is complete, assailed Christianity with most subtle reasoning, turned
it into a byeword and a joke ? Has

not Sir William Drummond, the most acute metaphysical critic of the age, a man of profound learning, high employment in the state, and unblemished integrity of character, controverted Christianity in a manner no less undisguised and bold than Mr. Paine? If Mr. Godwin in his *Political Justice* and his *Enquirer* has abstained from entering into a detailed argument against it, has he not treated it as an exploded superstition to which, in the present state of knowledge, it was unworthy of his high character as a moral philosopher, to advert? Has not Mr. Burton, a gentleman of great fortune, published a book called " Materials for Thinking" in which he plainly avows his disbelief in the divine authority of the Bible? Is not Mr. Bentham a Deist? What men of any rank in society from their talents are not Deists whose understandings have been unbiassed by the allurements of

worldly interest? Which of our great
literary characters not receiving emolument from the advocating a system of
religion inseparably connected with
the source of that emolument is not a
Deist? Even some of those very men
who are the loudest to condemn and
malign others for rejecting Christianity,
I *know to be Deists.* But that I disdain
to violate the sanctity of private intercourse for good, as others have done for
evil, I would state names.—Those already cited, who have publicly professed
themselves Deists, are the names of
persons of splendid genius, wealth and
rank, and exercising a great influence
thro' their example and their reasoning faculties upon the conduct and
opinions of their contemporaries. But
who is Mr. Carlile? A bookseller, I
imagine, of small means who with the
innocent design of maintaining his wife
and children took advantage of the
repeal of the acts against impugning the

Divinity of Jesus Christ to publish some books the main object of which was to impugn that notion and destroy the authorities on which it is founded. The chief of these works is the *Age of Reason*, a production of the celebrated Paine, which the prosecutors were so far unfortunate in selecting, whatever may be its defects as a piece of argument, inasmuch as it was written by that great and good man under circumstances in which only great and good men are ever found; at the bottom of a dungeon, under momentary expectation of death for having opposed a tyrant. It has the solemn sincerity, and that is something in an age of hypocrites, of a voice from the bed of death.

Why not brand other works which are more learned and systematically complete than this work of Paine's; why not brand works which have been

written not in a solitary dungeon, with
no access to any book of reference,
but in convenient and well-selected
libraries, by a judicial process? Why
not indict Mr. Bentham or Sir William
Drummond? Why crush a starving
bookseller and anathematize a work,
which though perhaps perfect enough
for its purpose, must from the very
circumstances of its composition be
imperfect? Surely, if the tyrants
could find any individual of the higher
classes of talent and rank, devoted to
the cause of liberty against whom from
any peculiar combination of accidents
they could excite the superstitions of
the people, no doubt they would
trample upon him to their heart's con-
tent, especially if circumstances permitted them to trample and to outrage
in secret. Tyrants after all are only a
kind of demagogues. They must
flatter the Great Beast. But in the

case of attacking any of the
aristocratical* Deists the risk of defeat
would be great, and the chances of
success, small. And the prosecutors
care little for religion, or care for it
only as it is the mask and the garment
by which they are invested with the
symbols of worldly power. In
persecuting Carlile, they have used the
superstition of the jury as their
instrument in crushing a political
enemy, or rather they strike in his
person at all their political enemies.
They know that the Established
Church is based upon the belief in
certain events of a supernatural
character having occurred in Judea
eighteen centuries ago ; that but for
this belief the farmer would refuse to
pay the tenth of the produce of his
labours to maintain its members in
idleness ; that this class of persons, if

* The word is not used in a bad sense ; nor is the
word " aristocracy " susceptible of an ill signification.
—Oligarchy is the term for the tyrannical monopoly of
the few. [Shelley's Note.]

not maintained in idleness, would have something else to do than to divert the attention of the people from obtaining a Reform in their oppressive Government, and that consequently the government would be reformed, and that the people would receive a just price for their labour, a consummation incompatible with the luxurious idleness in which their rulers esteem it their interest to live. —Economy, retrenchment, the disbanding of the standing army, the gradual abolition of the national debt by some just yet speedy and effectual system, and such a reform in the representation as by admitting the constitutional presence of the people in the state may prevent the recurrence of evils which now present us with the alternative of despotism or revolution, are the objects at which the jury unconsciously struck when from a sentiment of religious intolerance, they delivered a verdict of guilty against Mr. Carlile.   [P. B. Shelley.]